THE MAGICIAN OF CRACOW

1   2   3   4   5   79 78 77 76 75

Library of Congress Cataloging in Publication Data
(date)
Turska, Krystyna The magician of Cracow.
SUMMARY : A magician who wants to go to the moon sells
his soul to the devil to accomplish his objective.
[1.   Folklore—Poland.   2.   Devil—Fiction]   I.   Title.
PZ8.1.T8Mag3   [E]   75–8846   ISBN 0–688–80010–6   ISBN 0–688–84010–8 lib. bdg.

THE MAGICIAN
OF CRACOW

KRYSTYNA TURSKA

GREENWILLOW BOOKS
A DIVISION OF WILLIAM MORROW & COMPANY, INC.
NEW YORK

There once lived in Cracow a great magician who was famous all over Poland for his knowledge of spells and enchantments. Yet he never stopped studying and experimenting. However much he knew, he wanted to know still more. He was determined to become wiser and more powerful than any man in the world.

The secret he wanted most to discover was how to get to the moon. He tried every charm he could think of, until at last he was convinced that he would never find the answer by himself, and so he decided to risk a most dangerous spell.

He went to a mountain where he knew
the witches met. At midnight he stood alone
on the mountain-top and in his loudest voice
chanted the words of the spell.

As the last word rang out an elegant figure dressed all in black suddenly appeared beside him. It was the devil himself.

"You called me, master," the devil said, bowing low. "I am here."

"Good," said the magician. "Are you prepared to do whatever I ask?"

"Yes, I am," said the devil, "but only on the condition that when the time comes you will belong to me."

The magician hesitated a moment before he replied:

"I agree, but I have my own conditions. First, you must have granted me my dearest wish. And second, I must be in Rome at the moment when you take me away to do whatever you want with me."

Of course he meant to take good care never to set foot in Rome.

"I accept your conditions," said the devil, unwinding a roll of parchment. "Now sign this agreement."

The magician signed his name and the devil tucked the parchment safely away.

"I want you to start at once," the magician ordered. "Fetch all the silver there is in Poland and bring it to that cave down there on the mountain-side."

The devil summoned his assistants and they searched the whole country from the mountains to the sea, bringing loads of silver coins, ornaments and silver objects of all kinds to the cave.

By dawn the work was all done, and the devil wearily stood waiting for his master's next orders.

From a village far below came the sound of a cock crowing. It gave the magician a new idea.

"I want to travel all over the world," he said.

"Give me a strong cockerel that will carry me wherever I want to go."

At once a great cockerel appeared, ready bridled.

CRA COVIA

"To Cracow!" called the magician, jumping into the saddle.

The cockerel flew high into the air. Before long, the city with its church spires, narrow streets and crooked houses lay below them. The cockerel flew down to the market-place, and the townspeople hurried there to watch the magician dismount. Even the King himself came out of the palace to see why the crowds were cheering.

From then on the devil was kept busy bringing the magician jewels, magnificent clothes and treasures of every kind, and travelling with him to all parts of the world – except Rome, of course. The devil grew more and more tired of the magician's demands, which never stopped. He could see that only by tricking him would he be able to turn the tables and become the master instead of the servant.

On a wintry night, he disguised himself as a messenger from the King and drove in a sleigh to the magician's house. He knocked at the door. The magician looked out, and the messenger called up to him:

"The King commands you to come at once to his castle in the country and to bring with you your spells and magic medicines. The Princess is dangerously ill."

The magician got into the sleigh and they drove through the snow for many hours. At last, through the darkness, in the distance, they suddenly saw the light of an inn.

"Shall we stop at this inn to get warm and rest the horses?" asked the false messenger.

The magician was feeling cold and tired. He agreed and they stopped at the inn.

Its main room was crowded with people and full of smoke. Suddenly the messenger vanished and in his place stood the devil with a triumphant smile on his face. He pulled out the agreement the magician had signed on the mountain-top.

"Look at the name of this inn!" the devil said, pointing to a sign above the door.

Hardly able to believe his eyes, the magician read the word "ROME."

At that very moment the devil took hold of the terrified magician and flew right up the chimney with him, through the smoke, soot and cobwebs. Higher and higher they flew until there was nothing above them but the moon.

All of a sudden the magician remembered that in his excitement at being able to make the devil give him anything he wanted, he had forgotten to ask for the thing he longed for most of all.

"Stop!" he cried out. "There is one last task you must still do for me. You promised I could have my dearest wish before you took me away."

"I did," said the devil, "and I will keep my word. Give me your orders for the last time."

"I have not been to the moon," said the magician.

At that the devil gave a great shriek of disappoint-ment and vanished. For the devil of course is banned from all heavenly realms. The magician felt himself rushing through the air and closed his eyes in terror. When he opened them he found himself alone, sitting on the moon.

The magician knew that as long as he stayed on the moon, the devil could not harm him. So there he sits to this day. His only companion is a little spider which was caught in his cloak as they flew up the chimney of the inn called Rome.

Every now and then
the spider spins a thread down to earth.
He goes to Poland and visits the places
the magician used to know.
Then he comes back and brings news of Cracow to
the man on the moon.

The legend of the magician of Cracow grew up around the real-life career of a Polish nobleman, Pan Twardowski, who lived in Cracow in the 1500s and was a famous astronomer and alchemist. His learned interests and eccentric habits brought him fame (which increased through the ages) as a black magician with superhuman powers.

The original legend of Pan Twardowski, from which this story has been adapted, has acquired many variations, and become part of Polish folk-lore. In a widely accepted version the devil is vanquished by the power of prayer, remembered in the nick of time by the magician from the long-gone days of his childhood.